THORFINN THE NICEST VIKING

To Isaac and Martha – D.M.

To Dougie the doughnut muncher,
my faithful companion – R.M.

Kelpies is an imprint of Floris Books
First published in 2019 by Floris Books
Second printing 2019

 This book is also
available as an eBook

British Library CIP data available
ISBN 978-178250-565-5
Printed and bound by MBM Print SCS Ltd, Glasgow

MIX
Paper from
responsible sources
FSC® C117931

 Floris Books supports sustainable forest management
by printing this book on materials made from wood that
comes from responsible sources and reclaimed material

Thorfinn
and the
Dreadful Dragon

written by David Macphail
illustrated by Richard Morgan

HARALD THE SKULL-SPLITTER
CHIEF OF INDGAR

THORFINN THE
VERY-VERY-NICE-INDEED

MAGNUS THE
BONE-BREAKER

HEL THE
DRAGONSLAYER

NORWAY

THORFINN'S
JOURNEY

CHAPTER 1

When Vikings get together, it's usually for one of three reasons:

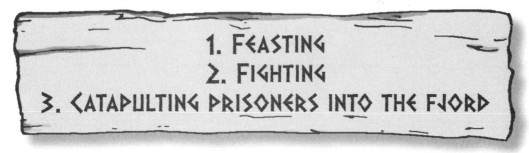

1. FEASTING
2. FIGHTING
3. CATAPULTING PRISONERS INTO THE FJORD

However, on this occasion, it was for a very unusual reason indeed.

The villagers of Indgar were gathered around a wooden stage set up in the marketplace. For Vikings, they were being amazingly well behaved.

No one was wrestling, farting, roaring, belching, sword fighting or arm-wrestling.

In fact, the villagers were rather quiet. There was a hushed kind of hubbub as they waited expectantly.

A small boy with freckles stepped up in front of the curtains. This boy had an extremely unusual name for a Viking. He was called Thorfinn the Very-Very-Nice-Indeed. If you're wondering what a normal Viking name sounds like, it would be more along the lines of Thorfinn the Tonsil-Mincer, or Thorfinn the Granny-Stretcher.

You see, Thorfinn was the exact opposite of all the other Vikings. Thorfinn was NICE, and he was POLITE, something which was unheard of in the mean and nasty world of the Vikings.

A pigeon perched on Thorfinn's shoulder, a lovely speckled bird that went by the name of Percy. He was equally well mannered (for a bird, anyway) and was one of Thorfinn's best friends. Gazing around at the gathered crowd, Thorfinn gave a pleasant smile and raised his helmet. "Good day to you all! And what a lovely morning!"

The crowd replied with a chorus of jeers and boos, followed by a volley of rotten cabbages. Vikings grew quite a lot of vegetables, but not for eating. It was much more fun to throw them at their enemies. And Thorfinn, obviously. "We're Vikings!" they roared. "We don't have lovely mornings, just horrible, smelly ones! Now get on with it!"

Thorfinn sidestepped the flying cabbages. He didn't flinch, and his gentle, well-meaning smile never faltered. "My dear friends," he said once a hush had descended on the crowd. "As you know, the Great Viking Fire Festival takes place on the Shetland Islands this week. We must look our best, so my father, the chief, has given me the great responsibility of making our costumes. My boat crew have kindly agreed to model them for you, so please give them a warm welcome!"

Thorfinn stretched out his arm. The curtain drew back, to reveal not his crew, but an ancient man with a long white beard. Or rather, an ancient man's rear end, because he was kneeling down, his bony bottom arched in the air towards the crowd, his head sideways on the floor. He was snoring loudly, like a giant hog snuffling in the feeding trough, and his beard ruffled in and out with each rasping breath.

It was Oswald, the village wise man.

"BOO!" cried the impatient crowd. "We want costumes, not bony old bums!"

Thorfinn coughed politely. "Excuse me, old friend."

Oswald woke up with a jolt. "Thorfinn!" he cried, sounding like a startled seagull. "Sorry! I bent down and couldn't get back up again. Must have dozed off while I was down there."

Thorfinn helped the old man to his feet, and Oswald hobbled offstage, muttering, "Ooh, my poor back!"

"Now, as I was saying," said Thorfinn, once again throwing out his arm to introduce his models.

"TA-DAAA!"

CHAPTER 2

One by one Thorfinn's crew trudged onto the stage. But there was nothing 'TA-DAAA' about them. They were led by Torsten the Ship-Sinker, Thorfinn's navigator. Unfortunately, the only ships he'd ever sunk were his own. With absolutely no sense of direction whatsoever, Torsten walked straight past Thorfinn and crashed off the side of the stage.

"AAARGH!"

Harek the Toe-Stamper, Thorfinn's chief warrior, followed close behind. He was the most accident-prone man in Norway, and put his foot through a plank in the floor.

CRACK!

He tugged his leg out, only to trip and fall off the stage, landing on top of Torsten.

"OW!"

"AIEEEEE!"

Then came Grut the Goat-Gobbler, munching on a gigantic chicken leg. His costume was bursting at the seams in an effort to contain his rather large behind, and he left an oily trail of chicken grease as it dripped all over the floor behind him.

Grimm the Grim trudged on next. Every part of the man was droopy – his face, his shoulders, even his moustache looked sad. He slipped on the grease from Grut's chicken and landed on his bottom, moaning, "Oh, this is so unfair. Why does it always happen to me?"

Grut bent over to hoist his friend up, but he slipped too, his legs scissoring in the air before he crashed onto his back. He managed to keep hold of his chicken leg, waving it aloft, shouting, "No one panic – I didn't drop it!"

The last member of the crew was the only one left standing: Gertrude the Grotty, Thorfinn's slimy-haired cook (the word 'cook' being used in the loosest possible sense). Her favourite ingredients were insects, which were usually found crawling, wriggling or buzzing all around her. Gertrude grinned and twirled her long straggly hair, posing for the crowd. "Finally I is on the catwalk," she screeched. "Look hows beautiful I am!"

A tiny red-haired girl wearing a helmet that was far too big for her stood at the side of the stage, one elbow propped up on the hilt of her giant axe. This was Velda, Thorfinn's other best friend. She rolled her eyes. "This is SOOOO embarrassing."

It takes a lot to make Vikings gasp, but gasp is what they did. A gasp full of shock and horror, like the winter wind whistling through a massive pair of Viking underpants hanging on the washing line.

But it wasn't the multi-Viking pile-up and greasy bums that did it. Oh no, it was the costumes.

Sparkly costumes. Sparkly and purple with shoulder pads and dangly, spangly tassels. And huge, tall hats made of fuzzy violet-coloured felt, all finished off with a sprinkle of glitter.

There was a moment of shocked silence from the crowd, before the wailing and pointing and shouting began. Not to mention the looks of murderous rage cast in Thorfinn's direction.

"THESE are the costumes?!"

"Is that... GLITTER?!"

"What have you done?" the crowd cried. "We'll be laughed out of the festival!"

One or two of the villagers sank to their knees in despair. A great cry went up as the shock turned to full-on outrage.

"Where's the shiny armour, Thorfinn?!" someone yelled.

"Where are the sharp swords?!"

"How are we supposed to look SCARY and TOUGH wearing sparkles and fuzzy felt?!"

"LET'S GET HIM!" someone cried. A mighty Viking roar came from the crowd as swords were drawn and axes were raised, until a booming voice halted them in their tracks.

"STOP!!"

CHAPTER 3

A giant, hulking figure
cast an enormous shadow
over the crowd. It was
Thorfinn's father, the
village chief, Harald the
Skull-Splitter.

Harald was one of the
toughest and meanest
Vikings in all Norway.
His skull-splitting skills
were the stuff of legend,

and he had been voted Most Terrifyingly Terrifying Viking of the Year six times in a row. Harald had an eye that twitched madly when he was angry, and a beard so huge you could hide weapons in it, which he often did.

"What is the meaning of this?" he bellowed.

"It's Thorfinn!" Erik the Ear-Masher pushed through the crowd. He was Harald's second in command. He only had one eye, and a nose like a mangled marrow. "Look at the horrible costumes he wants us to wear for the Great Fire Festival!"

"We can't wear those!" said Olaf, Erik's son, who elbowed his way to his father's side. Olaf had a nose just like his father's, except in his case the marrow was not only mangled, it had also been dropped from a great height, rolled around in the dirt for a bit, and then trampled by a horse. "We'll be a laughing stock!"

Onstage, the crew struggled to their feet. Thorfinn kindly helped Torsten and Harek back up the steps as Harald eyed the costumes with growing horror. "Thorfinn, explain yourself!"

"Father!" Thorfinn beamed with happiness.

He skipped off the stage and tipped his helmet.

"I'm so glad you could make it. And what a lovely—"

"YES, YES, YES – ENOUGH!" roared Harald. "I want you to explain this... **NONSENSE!**"

"Nonsense?" said Thorfinn. "I'm afraid I don't know what you mean, dear Dad."

"Now look, boy. The Great Fire Festival is the biggest event in the Viking calendar. Vikings from all over the world will be there, competing against each other."

"Yes, you said we have to put on a show." Thorfinn stretched out a hand towards his crew, who looked like fuzzy disco balls, and twiddled his fingers. "TA–DAAA!"

"Thorfinn," Harald growled, his eye twitching dangerously. "When I gave you the job of making

the costumes, I told you, very clearly, that you were

to make us look **FEROCIOUS!**"

"With a capital 'F'!" added Erik.

"And lots of RRRRRRR!" chipped in Olaf.

"And look what you've done," said Harald.

"People will think we're a comedy dance group!"

He spotted Velda, who was still propped on her axe. "You! This is all your fault!"

"Me?!" she protested.

"You're supposed to be keeping him out of trouble!" Harald had given Velda the job of coaching Thorfinn, hoping some of her fierce Viking spirit would rub off on his not-very-Vikingy son. It hadn't.

"I can't help it, he doesn't listen!" she replied.

"What'll we do now?" snarled Erik. "There's no way we're walking into the festival wearing T-T-TASSELS!" He gave a revolted shudder.

"We'll make new costumes," said Olaf.

"There's no time," grunted Harald, stroking his beard. "The festival starts in a few days, and we need to leave for Lerwick at high tide."

Erik drummed his fingers on his chin. "We could smear the costumes in mud," he said.

"Or dung," added Olaf.

"Or blood!" yelled someone from the crowd. "Thorfinn's blood!"

"LET'S GET HIM!" A loud cheer went up from the baying crowd once more.

But there was no time for Harald to calm them down, as just then a thunderous **BOOM** echoed from the direction of the village pier.

CHAPTER 4

All the villagers rushed towards the pier, led by Harald, but Velda soon overtook him. She was wearing furry ankle boots with tiny round logs strapped to the bottom. When she pushed against them, the logs spun round and propelled her along. She might not be the biggest or strongest Viking in Indgar, but now she was definitely the fastest.

"Hey, what are those things?" yelled Olaf.

"I call them roll-o-boots! Now out of the way, spud face!"

The pier was in pieces. In its place was the giant dragon-shaped prow of a huge longship, glimmering gold in the sunlight. The men hanging over the side wore shiny, expensive-looking armour, with even shinier winged helmets. They waved their swords around, jeering.

"Who do you think you are, smashing into my pier? Identify yourselves!" Harald's face was purple, his knuckles were clenched white around his sword hilt, and his eye was twitching like never before.

The leader of the crew, who was wearing an even larger and shinier helmet than the rest, grinned smugly.

"YOU!" cried Harald.

It was Magnus the Bone-Breaker, chief of the neighbouring village of Vennagar, and Harald's arch-enemy. "Ho, ho, ho! Look at your faces," laughed Magnus. "We're on our way to the Great Fire Festival. I just thought I'd pop by and show off our costumes. Brilliant, aren't they?" He gazed down admiringly at his own reflection in his wrist plates.

"PAH!" said Harald, but he was a terrible liar. The costumes were good. And tassel-free.

To make matters worse, someone on Harald's side was applauding them. Harald turned his twitchy eye back on the crowd. Whoever it was, he'd throw them into the nearest fjord! Thorfinn appeared, smiling and clapping his hands. Harald rolled his eyes and sighed. "I should have known..."

"Excuse me, my dear sir," said Thorfinn, "but they really are excellent costumes. What do you use to get them so wonderfully shiny?"

"Well I think they look ridiculous," said Velda, folding her arms angrily.

The rival chief ogled Thorfinn's crew – Torsten, Harek, Grut, Grimm and Gertrude – as they shuffled along behind the other villagers, still dressed in their spangly jackets and fuzzy purple hats. "Wait, are those *your* costumes?"

Harald's eye twitched.

"HA HA HA!" Magnus burst out laughing. So did his men, rolling around the ship in hysterics. "You look like the world's worst marching band! You've got no chance of winning the big prize!"

Harald's face looked like a volcano that was ready to erupt. "Well, neither have you, Bone-Breaker!" he growled.

"Oh no?" said Magnus, calmly inspecting his fingernails. "Just wait until you see my GRRRRR-AND finale. Or had you forgotten about that part?"

Harald looked sheepish.

"Grand finale? What does that mean?" demanded Velda.

"My big finish!" Magnus jabbed his sword down towards the ship's deck. "In order to win, you have to give the crowd a show: something amazing, a spectacle they've never seen before. Now imagine this fantastic longship, completely ablaze, and me and my men marching through the flaming embers. Ho, ho! We've got it all planned. They'll make me the Guizer Jarl for sure."

Thorfinn turned to Oswald, who was hunched on top of Harek the Toe-Stamper's shoulders. He had insisted on being carried down to the pier because of his bad back. "I beg your pardon, old friend, but I've never been to the Fire Festival before – what's a Guizer Jarl?"

"The Guizer Jarl is a position of great honour: Chief Viking," whined Oswald, sounding like an elk with a gobstopper in its mouth, "given to the chief who makes the finest display."

"You're going to set your own ship alight?!" scoffed Harald. "I always knew you had mashed turnip for brains, Bone-Breaker."

Magnus grinned smugly. "Oh, it'll be worth it for the title – plus, the winner gets a very large, very expensive silver mace. It'll look lovely sitting in pride of place in my feasting hall. We've just redecorated."

Harald went purple. "You'll never win, you festering pile of dung!"

"You wanna bet?" smirked Magnus. Winding up Harald the Skull-Splitter was one of his favourite hobbies (as well as knitting socks, but he didn't tell anyone about that).

"NO!" yelled Erik the Ear-Masher, tugging at Harald's mighty shoulder. "Don't bet anything with that trickster!"

Harald seethed, while Magnus and his men broke out in chicken impersonations, squawking and flapping their arms up and down. "Chicken! CHICK-CHICK-CHICK! Chicken!"

"Did someone say 'chicken'?" asked Grut, licking his lips.

Harald quivered with rage and went for his sword. "I'll run that rat through!"

"You can't do that, boss!" said Erik, holding him back. "Remember, there's a truce for the Fire Festival."

"Yes," piped up Oswald. "Any chief who breaks the truce forfeits his honour."

Harald glared at them for a second, before loosening his grip on his sword hilt. "Then I suppose I'd better WIN!" he thundered at Magnus. "I'll become Guizer Jarl, not you!"

"I bet you a hundred pieces of silver you don't!" Magnus called out gleefully.

Harald's eyes blazed and his nostrils flared. "Ha! You big shiny wimp! How about a thousand?"

Erik practically choked, while Magnus burst out in delighted laughter. "A thousand? You're on!" He turned to his crew and yelled, "Now cast off, pig-dogs!" The oarsmen pushed the longship away from the ruined jetty into the fjord. As the boat turned,

Magnus grinned and waved his sword at Harald and the assembled villagers of Indgar. "Cheerio, losers! I'll be back for my thousand pieces."

For the second time that morning, the villagers of Indgar stood in silent shock.

"A thousand pieces of silver!" said Olaf. "That's more than our whole village is worth."

Erik sank to the ground, his head in his hands. "Chief! What have you done?!"

CHAPTER 5

Later, in the great hall, the Vikings of Indgar sat slumped around the feasting table, their beardy chins propped upon their fists.

The long table stretched up the middle of the room, groaning under huge mounds of food, including leg of elk, fillet of reindeer, brisket of beef and roast partridge. This was their pre-voyage snack, but it was mostly untouched. None of them felt like eating. Even Grut the Goat-Gobbler seemed to have lost his usual appetite – all he'd eaten so far was half a wild boar, four roast chickens and a platter of venison sausages.

"This is the saddest feast ever," whined Grimm the Grim, casting his eyes up to the rafters. A weak flicker of a smile crossed his face. "I am SOOO happy."

Everyone was miserable, apart from Thorfinn of course, who was never sad. He sat next to his father, his knife, fork and spoon arranged in front of him, nibbling on a scone with jam and cream. He was humming and whistling cheerfully. "Dum-de-dum-dum..."

Percy perched on the table beside him, happily pecking up a few leftover crumbs.

"It's a lost cause, boss," grumbled Erik the Ear-Masher. "Not just because of Thorfinn's rubbish costumes. We can't afford a thousand pieces of silver. We'll lose the entire village to Magnus."

"Father's right," moaned Olaf. "How can we top a golden-prowed ship being set ablaze?"

"Oh, but I haven't told you about my secret plan for the big show!" said Harald, thumping the table.

"Would this secret plan involve us doing a Viking war dance?" muttered Velda.

"How did you guess?" barked Harald.

"Because it's what you always do when you don't have an *actual* plan. Surprise visit from the King? Do a Viking war dance. Forgot to get your wife a birthday present? Do a Viking war dance." Velda tutted. "You're lucky she didn't do her own war dance all over your face. Plus, we're rubbish at Viking war dances!"

Harald held his hands up. "Fine, I might have forgotten about the putting-on-a-show part, but if Magnus wins... How in the name of Thor's trousers can we raise a thousand pieces?"

"I know," said Olaf, brightening. "We could put Thorfinn in the village stocks and charge people to throw vegetables at him."

"NO!" yelled the chief.

"We could sell Thorfinn to those traders who passed by last week," chipped in Erik. "He'd make a fine slave, somewhere very exotic and *very* far away."

"NOOO!" boomed Harald. He sank his head into his hands and

45

sighed. "If we're going to stand any chance of keeping the village we need something big, something explosive, something that will blow Magnus and his stupid boat and silly costumes out of the water."

Harek sat nearby, lighting his pipe with a long taper. He blew it out, but a tiny cinder swirled in the air and landed on his thick bushy beard, which then burst into flames. "AAARGH!" he cried, trying to bat the flames down with his hand. "I'm on fire! HELP!"

Gertrude reached for a flagon of ale then tossed it over him, dousing the flames. "Sees?" she said smugly. "I is not just a pretty face, I is good in an emergency too!"

Watching the smoke drift up, Thorfinn took a thoughtful sip from his cup of pinecone tea. "Well, if we're going to the Shetland Islands anyway, we could always seek out the Great Dragon."

"What? What dragon?" asked Harald.

"If you're looking for something spectacular and fiery, then she might be able to help. My dear friend Oswald told me about her."

All eyes turned to Oswald, but unfortunately the old man was fast asleep, his head resting on Torsten the Ship-Sinker's shoulder. A trail of drool ran down his beard, and his mouth flapped open and shut with every whistling snore. **"ZZZZZZZ-weeeeeeee. ZZZZZZZ-weeeeeeee."**

"Wake him!" bellowed Harald.

Velda nudged Oswald with her axe but the old man didn't wake up.

"Hmm," said Thorfinn. "This may call for my delightfully strong tea." He flipped open a pouch on his belt and plucked out a small package wrapped in parchment.

"Your what?" asked Olaf. "It's only for use in emergencies, but it seems to do the trick." Thorfinn peeled open the paper wrapping and popped a pinch of tea leaves into a beaker of hot water. Then, very gently, he poured some of the tea into Oswald's open mouth.

Exactly two seconds later, Oswald's eyes shot open. The old man sprang into the air with a look

of shock on his face and
started doing star jumps,
his bad back forgotten.

"AAAARGH!"

he cried, unable to stop
himself.

"Nothing perks you up
like a nice cup of tea," said
Thorfinn, tucking the packet
back into his belt.

Once Oswald had calmed
down, Harald demanded
he tell them everything
he knew about the Great
Dragon of Shetland.

"A-ha," droned Oswald. "She was one of the last mighty sea dragons, ranging far and wide across the ocean. The Great Dragon lived on the remote clifftops on the northernmost tip of the Shetland Islands."

"Do you think she might help, old friend?" asked Thorfinn.

"She hasn't been sighted for ten years," he whined. "And neither has the great dragonslayer, Hel, who was her mortal enemy, and one of the fiercest Vikings ever to have lived. Hel used to battle the dragon across the length and breadth of the island chain. Stories of their terrific duels are told far and wide."

"What happened to them?" barked Harald.

"Many fear they both perished in the treacherous

waters around the islands. There are fierce whirlpools and strange-smelling blackened seas where most Viking ships fear to go."

Harald leaned forward. "Yet the dragon might still be alive?"

Oswald nodded.

Harald stroked his beard. "Hmm. It's a long shot."

"Long shot? It's the most ridiculous idea I ever heard!" Olaf cried.

"Even if we did somehow track down this dragon," added Erik, "why in Thor's name would it help us? And what's to stop it from burning us to a crisp?!"

Velda tossed aside the chicken leg she'd been munching on, wiped her mouth and belched before leaping to her roll-o-booted feet.

"An impossible mission, with almost zero chance of success. Ha! What are we waiting for?"

Thorfinn dabbed his mouth politely, folded his napkin and stood up, before tucking his stool neatly under the table. Percy fluttered up to perch on his shoulder. "Father, I'd be delighted to help. Or rather, my wonderful crew and I would. We'll set off at once."

Harald sighed and nodded. He had no other option. "Thorfinn, this is a truly desperate mission. But you are the cleverest of us all. If anyone can do it, you can."

Erik snorted. "Oh, come on! Surely you're not staking the future of our village on this crackpot scheme?!"

"And on Thorfinn?!" Olaf sneered.

"It seems no one has any better ideas," growled Harald, his eye twitching. He grasped his son by the shoulders. "Find the dragon. Persuade her to help us. Then meet us at the Fire Festival in Lerwick in three days' time."

CHAPTER 6

At the hastily mended pier, Thorfinn patted
the figurehead on his longship's prow, a green
dragon. "Let's go, old girl – a dragon in search of a
dragon."

Before Thorfinn could leap aboard, Harald
arrived to wave his son off. "Now, Thorfinn,
remember that the entire village is relying on you.
If you fail, we lose everything."

Thorfinn smiled up at him. "Of course, dear Dad.
Don't worry, I shall do my very best. I won't let you
down."

"And try not to get yourself barbequed by the blasted dragon," said Harald. "Your mother will kill me."

"Good luck!" cried Erik the Ear-Masher as Thorfinn hopped aboard to join the rest of his crew. "You'll need it, because it's a hopeless mission!" Then he pushed his son Olaf onto the boat just as they were about to cast off. "Sorry, son, but you're going too."

"What! You're sending me with these losers?!" complained Olaf.

"I need a real Viking on board to keep an eye on them," replied Erik.

Olaf stomped off to the back of the boat to sulk.

Meanwhile, Grut the Goat-Gobbler's stomach was rumbling. "I'm starving already. Any chance of something to eat?"

"I'm cookesin a nice beetle pie if yours interested," shrieked Gertrude. Grut, and indeed everyone else on the boat, quickly found something to keep them busy.

Everyone except Thorfinn, who smiled politely. "I'm afraid I don't eat insects, old friend."

"No," Gertrude said, grinning. "You is odd, but I forgives you."

Torsten the Ship-Sinker was scratching his head, staring at a map spread out in front of him. "Now, which way's the sea?"

Velda snatched the map, turned it the right way up, then pointed behind his shoulder. "See that big blue wet thing over there? That's the sea. Now get on with it!" She skated around the deck in her roll-o-boots, hoisting the sails and manning the steering tiller. "Out of my way, cretins!" she yelled, nudging Harek. But she underestimated her speed and Harek crashed overboard.

"AAAAARGH!"

"I have a very bad feeling about this trip," moaned Grimm the Grim as he lassoed his crewmate with a rope and hauled him back onboard.

"Huh! You're not the only one," grumbled Olaf.

Oswald blew the dust off a thick brown book he had pulled from his cloak. "Here, Thorfinn, you'll need this if we're to find the Great Dragon."

"You want to track down a dragon using a silly old book?" said Olaf.

"You'll find that books are useful tools in any situation," replied Oswald.

"Rubbish! Can you win battles with them? Can you crush the skulls of your enemies with them?"

Oswald calmly leaned over and clobbered Olaf over the head with the heavy tome. "Sometimes, if needed," he whined.

Olaf was very quiet after that.

Thorfinn took the leather-bound book from Oswald and turned it over in his hands, gazing at it in wonder. "*The Book of Dreki*," he said, reading the rune writing on the cover.

"*The Book of Dragons*," translated Oswald.

"It was written by the great Oslo the Dragon-Feeder. It contains everything we Vikings know about dragonkind – information about the different species, where they live, what they eat, what to do if one chomps off your head – you know, all the need-to-know stuff."

Despite Torsten setting off in the wrong direction then reversing into some moored longships, they eventually managed to make their way out of the fjord. They were soon headed towards the west and the setting sun.

"Next stop, the Shetland Islands," called Thorfinn. **"HUZZAH!"** cried the crew.

CHAPTER 7

Over the next two days they forged through rough seas and icy winds. On the third morning the weather grew even colder. Thorfinn wrapped a scarf around his neck and Percy huddled on his shoulder for warmth. He opened up *The Book of Dreki*. "According to the book's map, we should be nearing the northernmost tip of the Shetland Islands. It says, **'HERE RANGES THE GREAT SEA DRAGON AND HER KIND.'**"

"What's that?" cried Velda, pointing out a dark stretch of water filling the horizon on their right.

"Aha!" said Thorfinn. "That is what they call **THE BLACKENED SEA**. It's here on the map."

"The water there is strange and black," explained Oswald. "Vikings believe it is cursed, for many ships have been lost there, disappearing or suddenly bursting into flames for no reason."

The crew's faces were pale as they stared at the mysterious patch of water.

"Hmm. We'd best steer clear of it," said Thorfinn, and the crew sighed with relief.

"Wait!" called Harek. "Up ahead, look!"

They heard a roaring noise, like a great storm.

A vast, swirling mass of water lay directly in their path. It was a giant whirlpool, with white foam frothing from the centre.

"They call it the Corrydreki," croaked Oswald. "It will tear our ship apart!"

"Oh! That's on my map too," called Thorfinn, cheered to see his map was entirely accurate.

"There's no way past it!" shouted Velda.

"We're DOOOOOOMED!" wailed Grimm.

"Any chance of a final meal before we die?" asked Grut, licking his lips.

"How abouts a lovely dung beetle omelette?" said Gertrude.

Grut flung his arm over Grimm's shoulder and joined in the wailing. "We're DOOOOOOMED!"

Thorfinn paused in thought for a second, the whirlpool looming closer and closer. He licked his finger and held it up in the air. Then he calmly stepped up onto a barrel and coughed politely. "My dear friends," he said, "would you be so good as to man the oars?"

"Are we going back?" Olaf asked hopefully.

"I'm afraid not, and the wind's too strong for us to cut to the left. We'll have to take our chances on **THE BLACKENED SEA**."

Olaf gulped. "What?! Are you mad? It's cursed, didn't you hear?"

"Shuddup and get rowing, spud features!" yelled Velda.

Everyone grabbed an oar and started rowing to the right. Except Torsten, who pulled to the left.

"Oh, sorry, my bad!" he said, before pulling the same way as everybody else.

The boat turned, slowly but surely, away from the thrashing waves of the whirlpool and towards the dreaded waters of the Blackened Sea.

CHAPTER 8

The crew of the *Green Dragon* leaned over the side of the ship, gazing fearfully at the water's dark surface.

Velda sniffed the air, which had a strange and stinky whiff. "Phew! What's that awful smell?"

"Whatever it is, it's put me right off my food," said Grut, rubbing his stomach.

"Who fancies a snail baguette?" said Gertrude.

"That's also put me off my food," added Grut.

"Dear pals, I'm sure there's nothing to fear. Perhaps a little bit of research is in order," said Thorfinn thoughtfully. He snatched a cup and turned to Harek. "Pardon me, dear friend, but would you mind swinging me over the side?"

Velda turned to Harek, holding her axe up to his face. "Don't you dare drop him, you butter-fingered oaf!"

Harek shrugged and did as he was told, dangling Thorfinn just above the sea's surface. Reaching out, Thorfinn scooped up a cup of the strange black water.

"Would you mind terribly pulling me up now, please?" he called, and Harek hoisted him back on board.

Once upright, Thorfinn dabbed his finger in the liquid, sniffed it, then tasted it with his tongue. He nodded. "Yes, it's a kind of oil. Thick, black oil."

"Of course! It seeps up from the sea bed," said Oswald. "It's highly flammable. No wonder ships burst into flames."

"As long as we don't light any fires then it shouldn't trouble us," said Thorfinn.

They turned to find Gertrude lighting a fire in the brazier.

"NOOOO!"

Velda sped over on her roll-o-boots and emptied a bucket of water over it.

"Whats did you do that for?!" shrieked Gertrude. "I was just abouts to cook."

"In that case, I just saved the crew's life twice over," said Velda.

They soon spotted lighter-coloured sea on the horizon, and everyone on board held their breath until they crossed into it.

Grimm stared up at the skies, his eyes wet with tears. "I'm alive! I promise I'll never moan again!"

At that exact moment, a giant seagull poo splattered across his helmet and down his shoulder. "Oh, why does everything ALWAYS happen to me?!" he wailed.

Slowly, a coastline appeared on the horizon. They sailed round a headland into a sheltered bay, fringed by a ramshackle village with a jetty jutting out into the water. The village was dwarfed on either side by humungous jagged cliffs.

Thorfinn flipped open *The Book of Dreki*. "Hmm, it says here that the tall sea cliffs in this region are the great sea dragon's favourite habitat, but there do seem to be an awful lot of them round here... Perhaps the locals can point us in the right direction."

CHAPTER 9

The crew tied the *Green Dragon* up at the jetty. Thorfinn went ashore with Olaf, Velda, Harek and Grimm. Oswald insisted on coming too, but as his 'bad back' had mysteriously returned he demanded to be carried. Grimm and Olaf heaved the old man onto Harek's back as Oswald whined, "Hurry up, you dung merchants!"

They made a strange sight as they crossed the village, with Percy perched on Thorfinn's shoulder, Harek carrying Oswald, Velda on her roll-o-boots and Grimm moping along behind. Olaf heaved a long painful sigh, and shook his head. "What *do* we look like?!"

Oswald replied by snatching the dragon book out of Thorfinn's hands and whacking Olaf over the head with it.

"OUCH!"

Leading the way, Thorfinn came to a stop outside the village inn. "Shall we start our enquiries here, old friends?"

He strolled inside with his crew following behind him and ambled up to the bar, tipping his helmet to the barman. "Good day, my dear sir!"

The barman, a great barrel-chested man, took in the smiling, freckly boy with a pigeon on his shoulder. Then the rag-tag group of misfits behind.

His mouth fell open.

"Yeah, I know," said Velda. "Just roll with it."

Thorfinn continued: "I don't suppose you've seen any dragons in these parts?"

The man laughed, a great booming guffaw that rattled the flagons on the shelf behind him.

"Ha! Well, if it's dragons you're after, why don't you try that bloke sitting in the corner there." He pointed at a sad-looking man slumped at a table. He had a drooping moustache, and stared down glumly into his flagon of mead.

Thorfinn approached, flanked by his crew. "Good day. I understand that you might be the person to speak to about dragons?"

The big man sniffed. "I was once. Now, I'm not so sure."

"We're looking for the one they call the Great Dragon?"

"You won't have much luck. She hasn't been seen for ten years." He emptied the contents of his flagon down his throat and belched. "I should know, I was the last one who saw her."

Oswald suddenly gave Harek a swift kick. "Put me down, you stinking oaf!" Once on solid ground, he leaned forward to peer into the miserable man's face. "It can't be ... but it is!"

"Who?" asked Velda.

"He was so fearless. It is said that even the King had a portrait of him in his great hall," Oswald droned. "Huh! And now look at him."

"Who?" Velda repeated.

"Heartbreaking!" added Oswald, with a shake of his head.

"WHO? WHO?" cried Velda.

"All this suspense is SO depressing!" blubbed Grimm.

"Why, it's Hel, the greatest, most fearsome dragonslayer of them all. Slayed every dragon he ever fought – except one."

"Him?!" cried Velda, staring in horror at the man's greying hair, tattered furs and rusty sword.

"Yes, that was me." Hel's eyes glistened as he gazed off into the distance. "Whole towns used to watch in amazement as I battled that pesky dragon. People cheered in their hundreds as I pursued her in my golden-wheeled chariot... or my trusty longship, *Dragonsbane*. With my flaming sword, I chased

her away from
many a village.
Everywhere
I went people
chanted my
name. Ah, those
were the days."

"But why did
she disappear?" asked Thorfinn.

Hel shrugged. "No idea. We'd just fought a very

long and epic duel. The skies thundered as we

traded blows. Then she gave a sort of cough and

a splutter, and wheeled into the clouds. That was

the last I ever saw of her. Not even a card on my

birthday." Hel's face crumpled, and he started to cry.

"BOO HOO! I miss her!"

"You know, I'm starting to like this man," said Grimm, patting the dragonslayer on the shoulder.

"My dear sir, can I ask where you last saw her?" asked Thorfinn, producing a clean handkerchief and passing it to the weeping former warrior.

"Off the cliffs," said Hel pointing, before blowing his nose loudly. **HONNNNK!** "Way to the west of here. A sparse, rocky and uninhabited stretch of coast."

Thorfinn turned to his crewmates and smiled. "Then what are we waiting for, my good friends?"

"Wait!" sniffed Hel. "Are you going to try and track her down?"

"Why, yes," said Thorfinn.

"You won't find her." He shook his head, then

grabbed Thorfinn's sleeve. "But if you do, then you'd better watch out! She's the most ferocious dragon I ever fought. Her teeth are as sharp as sabres. Her eyes blaze like the heat of a volcano. And her breath is hotter than a barbeque in hell."

"Yum, barbeque," said Grut dreamily.

"She'll burn you to a cinder before you even blink," continued the dragonslayer. "Then she'll gobble you up in a heartbeat and eat your friends here for pudding."

Grimm started blubbing. "I might have known I'd end up as some great monster's pudding. Oh poor me!"

"You really *are* a pudding!" shouted Velda. "Now get a move on! We need to find this dragon. The entire village of Indgar depends on it!"

CHAPTER 10

Thorfinn and the crew set sail, hugging the rugged coastline to the west. The clifftops soared high above them, and seabirds swooped and dived around their heads.

"Why would a dragon disappear?" Velda asked.

"What does *The Book of Dreki* say, Thorfinn?" asked Oswald.

Thorfinn flicked open the book and ran his finger along the crusty yellow pages. "It says, **'WHEN ILL OR UNHAPPY, DRAGONS WILL OFTEN RETREAT TO A CAVE IN A REMOTE SPOT.'**"

"You think the dragon is hiding in a cave somewhere?" asked Velda.

"Hel said she gave a sort of cough and then disappeared. It seems rather odd that he mentioned it, so yes, perhaps the dragon was ill," replied Thorfinn.

"But how do we find this cave?" Velda stared up at the surrounding rocks.

Thorfinn continued reading: "**'LOOK OUT FOR SCORCH MARKS FROM THEIR HOT BREATH, OR SCRATCH MARKS AT THE CAVE MOUTH. DRAGONS ALSO SHED THEIR SCALES, WHICH THEY CAST ON THE GROUND OUTSIDE'.**"

Thorfinn pulled out his spyglass and peered through it, searching the cliffs for any sign of the dragon. "Aha!" He handed it to Velda and pointed in the direction of a black cave sitting atop the highest cliff stack. "See the reddish colour on the ground, spreading out from the cave's mouth?"

"Could be dragon's scales," said Oswald.

"My thought exactly," said Thorfinn cheerfully. "Let's go up there and see."

"Woah! Woah! Woah!" Olaf waved his arms. "You heard that man Hel. That dragon's ferocious, he said. I distinctly remember the words 'burn' and 'cinder'."

"Oh, I'm sure she won't hurt us," replied Thorfinn. "Not if we're perfectly nice to her. After so much time alone, she'll be overjoyed to have visitors."

Olaf stomped off in a huff. "Yeah, I'm sure that empty stomach of hers will be thrilled to see us!"

They pulled in at a tiny cove, the bow of the longship crunching against the pebbly beach. Thorfinn, Harek and Grut leapt over the side, while Velda slung her roll-o-boots over her shoulder for the climb.

Gertrude waved them off. "I'll haves a tasty snack

ready for yous ifs – I mean, *whens* – you comes back. A lovely boiled beetle stew!"

Olaf glowered at them from his spot near the prow. He had refused to come on account of not wanting to become a tasty snack himself.

"I thought you were a real Viking?" asked Velda with a grin.

"Yeah, a real *live* one, and I want to stay that way!" huffed Olaf.

The group were just starting to clamber up a track that led towards the cliffs when there was a whine like a slowly deflating balloon. "Hey, wait! You're not leaving me here with these turnip heads!" Oswald shook his fists and yelled at Harek and Grut, "You must carry me, you bilge rats!"

"No chance, you old goat!" yelled Grut.

"Yes," he insisted. "Or I'll put pigeon poo in your ale!"

Harek and Grut stared fearfully at each other, then glanced at Percy, who was perched on the ship's rail. Percy seemed to shrug.

"Tchoh! Alright!" snapped Harek. He and Grut argued over who would do the carrying. Being Vikings, they didn't have any straws to draw, so they pulled beard hairs instead.

"**OUCH!** Ha! Mine is longer!" cried Harek. "You have to carry the old windbag!"

Grut sighed as he hoisted Oswald over his back. "I'd better get double rations for this!"

Thorfinn and Velda forged ahead. The track became steeper until it cut through a narrow gap in the rocks. Soon, they were standing on top of the cliffs, staring down at the longship below. The mouth of the cave was only a short distance away, and up close, the ground was clearly covered in reddish scales. Thorfinn picked one up and turned it over in his fingers. It was as hard as plate armour. He stepped up to the edge of the dark cave and called inside. "Hello in there!"

His voice echoed back at him: "...lo in there!...

O in there!… O in there!"

"You absolutely sure this is a good idea?" whispered Velda out of the side of her mouth.

But Thorfinn didn't get a chance to answer.

Suddenly, deep in the blackness, something stirred.

CHAPTER 11

A pair of slitted yellow eyes cracked open in the dark and glared out at Velda and Thorfinn. A blast of hot, foul-smelling air blew the helmets off their heads. Then came a low, slithery growl, followed by a fierce but somehow frail voice. "Who are you, to enter *my* cave?"

Thorfinn stepped forward and smiled politely. He was going to doff his helmet – except that it had been blown off and lay about two longship-lengths behind him. "Oh, good day. My name is Thorfinn. I'm ever so sorry to bother you, but I represent the

Vikings of Indgar."

Another growl, and the voice spoke again:
"Thhh-orfinn, hmmm? I wonder what a Thhh-orfinn
tastes like?"

Velda stretched out her leg and took a LOOONG
step away from her friend.

The lizardy eyes loomed closer. A head poked
out of the shadows, a giant head, with a hard,
shiny nose. Its teeth were just as sharp as Hel had
described. Its scales were a deep red, and two large
claws reached out, each so huge they would make
Harald the Skull-Splitter look like a teeny-weeny
beardy flea in comparison.

The dragon's belly rumbled, a sound so low that
even the pebbles on the ground began to vibrate.

Grut, who'd just struggled up the steep slope carrying Oswald on his back, and Harek both froze. Oswald had been napping, but now he sprang awake. "Oh my great giddy Thor!"

Thorfinn moved closer, smiling. "Pardon me, but would you by any chance be the Great Dragon?"

The dragon's eyes flickered with surprise. "The Great Dragon... Yessss, that is what they used to call me.

Mmmany years ago... These islands were *my* islands. People would gaze up at me in terror assss I roamed the skies. I used to have such great battles with their dragonsssslayer, Hel. Oh, how I missss those dayssss!"

"Oh dear! I am sorry," said Thorfinn. "Can I ask what happened to you, dear friend?"

"I caught a cold," the dragon said sadly.

"So you were right, Thorfinn!" said Velda.

The dragon coughed – probably quite a gentle cough for a dragon, but to everyone else it sounded like a siege cannon blasting the walls off a fort. And it felt even worse than it sounded, as the shockwave blew everyone off their feet. Grut teetered for a moment, then fell back.

"You rollicking oaf!" yelled Oswald as they both tumbled back down the slope.

Grut's moans echoed around the cliffs as he bounced down the rocks. **"OW. OW, ow, OW, OW. ow."**

The cough also set off a cascade of metal in the cave's darkness. Behind the dragon lay mounds of silver and gold and jewels. Once upon a time they might have gleamed and sparkled, but now they were dull and covered in dust.

Ever the Viking, Velda's eyes gleamed. "Look at all that lovely loot!"

"My dear friend, I wouldn't recommend you touch it," said Thorfinn. "*The Book of Dreki* says dragons get very attached to their treasure."

The dragon sniffled, and Velda's brow creased as she stood up. "You've had a cold that's lasted ten years?" she asked.

"A dragon'sss cold can last decades. I just cannot shhhake it off. Oh, it's drrreadful! I can't even breathe fire any more."

The dragon arched her neck, as if about to spew forth great flames, but instead gave a mighty

sneeze. Thorfinn and Velda both ducked. A giant
spurtle of greeny goo flew out of her nose. Harek
dodged out of its way in the nick of time, only to
find that he'd rather dodged into its way instead.

Harek sprawled flat on his back, smothered in slimy dragon snot. Meanwhile, Grut had scrambled back up the slope for the second time, panting and carrying Oswald over his shoulders. Grut stared down at his friend and whistled. "I'm glad I drew the short hair."

The dragon sighed, a long, sad sigh full of misery. "I am no longer the Grrreat Dragon. I'm jussst plain old Hazel."

"Hazel?" asked Thorfinn.

"Hazel wasss my original name. Oh yesss, we all have normal names, we dragonsss. My ffffather was Edward, my mother was Jennifer."

"Well," said Thorfinn. "I think Hazel is a perfectly lovely name, and I intend to call you that from now on."

He stepped closer and gently placed his hand on Hazel's nose.

Velda gasped. "Thorfinn, be careful!"

But Hazel let him pat her. She even leaned towards him a little bit, like a very scaly, very overgrown cat. "You poor, poor thing," said Thorfinn. "Tell me, my dear friend, can your cold be cured?"

"Oh, if only sssomeone could," Hazel sniffled. "I would be indebted."

Thorfinn scratched his chin. "Hmm, what if I was able to help you? What if I could not only make you well again, but make you *great* again? And if I could do that, might you be willing to do us a little favour?"

The edges of the dragon's mouth turned up, almost like a smile. "My dear Thhh-orfinn," she said. "If you could do all that, why, I might not eat you after all."

CHAPTER 12

With a grunt and a heave, the Vikings launched their longship off the beach.

"Phew!" said Velda. "I'm glad to get away from that dragon. But where now?"

"Yeah, and how in Valhalla are we supposed to cure a dragon's cold?" sniped Olaf.

Grut scratched his head. "Well, you know the old saying, 'Feed a cold, starve a fever'? Actually, I feel a bit sniffly myself. Any chance of some lunch?"

"I haves a special soup that gets rid of coughs and sneezes," shrieked Gertrude. "It's cream of cockroach."

Grut gulped. "Suddenly I feel a lot better."

"Why don't we make Hazel a hot toddy?" suggested Velda.

"What's in it? Whisky, fruit, honey?" asked Olaf. "Do we even have any of those things?"

"No, the whisky ran out days ago," called Torsten from the steering tiller. "We used it to fumigate Oswald's underpants."

"How dare you!" whined the old man, sounding like a donkey with tonsillitis.

"How about honey?" asked Velda.

"You must be joking!" said Torsten. "Grut polished that off half an hour after we left Indgar."

"And fruit?" added Olaf hopefully.

Torsten burst out laughing. "HAAAAAA! Next

you'll be asking if we eat vegetables!"

"No hot toddy, then. So what in Odin's name are we going to do?" cried Olaf. "Harald and the rest of the village are expecting to meet us in Lerwick tonight with a dragon that breathes fire, not germs!"

Gertrude jabbed her thumb at Harek, who was sitting on a barrel staring into space. He had cleaned off most of the dragon snot, but he still looked quite gooey. "What's up with him?"

"The dragon sneezed on him," explained Velda.

"Lucky so-and-so!" gasped Gertrude. "Dragon snot is quite tasty so I hears."

Thorfinn, who'd been flicking through *The Book of Dreki*, neatly stepped up onto a barrel. "Excuse me, my dear friends. Here it says:"

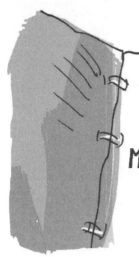

FOR A DRAGON'S COLD, GIVE **BLACK OIL**, MEASURED BY THE BUCKET, FOR AS LONG AS SYMPTOMS PERSIST.

"But where will we get that?" asked Velda.

"Simple." Thorfinn turned to Torsten the Ship-Sinker. "My dear friend, would you please set sail to the east."

Torsten cringed. "Er..."

"Oh, sorry, I mean that way, dear pal." Thorfinn smiled and pointed in the direction of the dark patch of water on the horizon. "Towards the Blackened Sea."

As they sailed into the black, murky water once again, the crew peered over the side of the ship into the inky gloop below.

"This is never going to work," scoffed Olaf. "You'd need loads of oil to cure something the size of a dragon."

Undeterred, Thorfinn turned to Gertrude. "Pardon me, old friend. Would you mind terribly lending me a cauldron and a soup ladle, please?"

The cook paused for a second. "OK, but only cos you asked so nicely."

Once Thorfinn had explained his plan to the crew, they lowered him over the side of the longship with a rope tied around his waist. He whistled cheerily as he wielded a long stick with Gertrude's soup ladle lashed to the end. Velda dangled next to him,

cradling a bucket in the crook of her elbow. As they splashed through the waves, Thorfinn skimmed his ladle across the oily surface, then dolloped the black oil into Velda's bucket.

"Excellent work!" cheered Oswald, sounding like a gannet that had just swallowed a very large fish.

Olaf stared wide-eyed over the side as the bucket began to fill up. "I don't believe it! It's actually working!"

"Of *course* it is, you festering pig-dog!" cried Velda from the end of the rope.

The bucket was soon full, and Grut hauled it aboard before tipping it into Gertrude's big cooking cauldron on deck. They did this again and again until the cauldron was filled to the brim. "There we have it, medicine for Hazel," said Thorfinn cheerfully.

"But Thorfinn," said Velda. "The Great Fire Festival takes place tonight. We don't have enough time to cure Hazel and get to Lerwick."

In reply, Thorfinn just smiled. Then he asked Torsten to turn the ship around and drop him off at the beach.

"I'll take the medicine up to Hazel and meet you at the festival," he said. "You should head straight there, but would you mind awfully picking up Hel the Dragonslayer on the way?"

"Why? What's your plan, Thorfinn?" Velda asked.

"We're going to bring a legend back to life, old friend. Is there a bigger or better show than that?"

CHAPTER 13

As the prow of the longship crunched into the sand of the dragon's cove, Thorfinn pushed himself off the side, landing on the beach. Grut winched off the cauldron of oil and Harek tossed a very long rope and a pulley at Thorfinn's feet. "Good luck, Thorfinn," he boomed.

"CAST OFF, YOU SLOTHS!" screamed Velda, and the *Green Dragon* pushed away from the shore.

Thorfinn raised his helmet. "Good day, my dear friends. I shall see you this evening."

Alone except for Percy, Thorfinn scaled the cliff with the rope wound round his shoulder, then rigged up his pulley at the very top. Percy watched as Thorfinn cleverly heaved the cauldron up the sheer rock face, the thick oil slopping over the sides. Whistling, he plonked the cauldron down outside Hazel's cave and called inside. "Pardon me, dear Hazel?"

A pair of yellow eyes opened in the darkness, and the outline of a scaly body uncurled around a great mound of treasure. "Thhh-orfinn, I did not expect to see you again so sssoon," said the dragon.

"I've returned with some medicine for you, as promised."

Hazel gulped down the contents of the cauldron. "Ah, that feelsss better already," she gasped.

It didn't take long, perhaps a few minutes, before her tummy rumbled and tendrils of smoke began to wisp out of her huge nostrils.

"Duck, my little Thhh-orfinn," said Hazel gently.

Seeing the dragon's mouth opening and a fire kindling in her throat, Thorfinn threw himself to the ground, grabbing Percy. A ferocious blast of fire thundered over their heads.

When Thorfinn looked up again, Hazel was a different dragon altogether. The sad look was gone from her eyes, replaced by a fierce, fiery glint.

"Thhh-orfinn, I feel fffantastic! Just like my old ssself again! However can I repay you?"

Thorfinn smiled. "Well, dear pal, do you remember that favour I mentioned?"

CHAPTER 14

Lerwick's Great Fire Festival was one of those few
occasions when Vikings got together for reasons
other than fighting.

The town itself was made up of a jumble of
wooden houses clustered around a bay. The narrow
streets and harbourside were crowded with Vikings,
all wearing different costumes. There were Scottish
Vikings wearing tartan and doing the Highland fling,
Russian Vikings wearing bearskins and Cossack-
dancing, and English Vikings wearing monocles and
shouting 'I say' a lot, adding 'RAAR!' afterwards to

remind everyone they were still Vikings (and jolly fierce ones too).

Local market traders were selling everything from barbecued meat to souvenir helmets with drinking horns attached. There was a fair too, and a Ferris wheel powered by a Highland cow. Vikings crammed onto it, singing songs in their great booming voices as it turned, while stuffing their faces with barbecued chicken legs.

Thorfinn's father, Harald the Skull-Splitter, cast a twitchy eye over the crowd from his spot on the harbour wall, then gazed up at the darkening sky. It would soon be nightfall, when the festival would really start. And there was no sign of Thorfinn and his crew.

A huge horn sounded, and Harald turned, along with everyone else, to see his rival chief Magnus the Bone-Breaker leading his team of men up a slipway. Wearing their shiny armour, they heaved the boat ashore, bringing it to a halt at a prime spot beside some big rocks, backing onto the sea's lapping waves. A crowd started to gather around them.

"Skull-Splitter!" called Magnus. "I hope you brought your silver with you. When they see this ship going up in flames they're going to make me the Guizer Jarl for sure!"

Harald's second in command, Erik the Ear-Masher, came rushing through the crowd, breathless. "We're ready, boss!"

"Good," barked Harald. He had men waiting to spring open the gate of the market's cattle pen. A nice stampede would hold things up for a while and maybe buy Thorfinn enough time to get there.

"Where's that son of yours got to?" barked Erik. Which was exactly what Harald was thinking. If he didn't appear soon they'd be in trouble.

A moment later, a tiny figure of a girl with red hair wheeled her way through the bustling crowd, dodging, ducking and swerving. She gave several kneecaps a good thwack with her axe handle when their owners failed to move fast enough.

"You're here!" yelled Harald with relief.

"Wotcha, Chief!" answered Velda.

"But where's Thorfinn? And who is this decrepit fool?" He jabbed his thumb at the giant man with a droopy moustache who trailed behind her.

"This..." Velda leaned forward, put her finger to her lips, then whispered, "is Hel the Dragonslayer."

"HEL THE DRAGONSLAYER?"

bellowed Harald at the top of his voice.

Velda slapped her hand against her forehead. "Big secret, Chief!"

"Sorry!" Harald added, but it was too late. The words 'HEL' and 'DRAGONSLAYER' were passing quickly through the gathered crowd.

"Look!" said someone. "Is that Hel?"

"The Dragonslayer? He's here?" gasped another.

"Well," said Erik the Ear-Masher with a sigh, "it's
not a secret now!"

Harald silenced him with a stare from his
twitchy eye, then turned back to Hel. "You must be
joking! This wet fish, the famous dragonslayer?!"

But even as he spoke, Hel was transforming. His shoulders straightened, his chest puffed out, and even his moustache perked up.

"YES," came Hel's booming voice. "I am he, the famous dragonslayer!"

The crowd pressed forward, moving away from Magnus and his men, and instead crowding round Hel to get a good look at the unexpectedly returned hero.

Magnus eyed Harald angrily, muttering to himself, "What are you up to, Skull-Splitter? Hmm, I'm going to make sure you can't ruin my big show..."

Harald turned again to Velda. "But where's Thorfinn?"

"He said to meet him here," said Velda. "He was going to bring the..." She hushed her voice as she began spelling out, "D.R.A.G.O.N."

Spelling had never been Harald's strong point (he liked battles, not books), so it took him a while to work out what she was saying.

"DRAGON!"

Velda slapped her forehead again and Erik rolled his eyes. Now the word 'DRAGON' started echoing through the excited crowd.

"Has the Great Dragon returned?" said someone.

"Is that why Hel's here?" guessed another.

The clamour increased until the crowd seemed

to swallow Hel up. People were asking for his autograph and chanting his name.

At that moment, the rest of Thorfinn's crew appeared, pushing their way through the horde of Vikings.

Harek and Grut had grown tired of carrying Oswald, so they'd 'borrowed' a wheelbarrow from one of the local market traders. They were thoroughly enjoying steering him over the bumpiest bits of path. "Careful, you lumbering cretins!" the old man whined.

Olaf stepped up next to his father, Erik, and tutted loudly. "Thorfinn will never make it. This crackpot scheme of his was hopeless from the start!"

Oswald sighed, and pulled out *The Book of Dreki* from the folds of his cloak. He leaned over and whacked Olaf on the head with it. "It is thanks to Thorfinn that we even have a plan. Even I didn't think it was possible. Yet Thorfinn tracked the Great Dragon down."

"Yeah, while the REAL Vikings like you were hiding aboard the ship," mocked Velda.

"So how long are we supposed to wait?" growled Erik. "If Thorfinn doesn't arrive soon, we're going to lose the village to Bone-Breaker and his barbequed boat!"

"Forget Thorfinn, we have another problem," said Velda.

"What?" growled Harald.

Velda nodded at the swarming crowd of Vikings. Hel was nowhere to be seen. "We've lost the dragonslayer."

CHAPTER 15

"WHHEEEEEEE!"

Thorfinn giggled as Hazel swooped through the sky, skimming the white fluffy cloud tops. He was perched on her enormous back, one hand holding on tight, the other clutching his helmet.

"How do you like flying, Thhh-orfinn?" Hazel called back.

"I think it's a delightful way to travel," replied Thorfinn.

Hazel sucked in a great lungful of air and sighed. "Fff-inally, I fff-eel like my old ssself again!"

"Do you think we can make it to Lerwick in time, my dear friend?" asked Thorfinn.

"I'll try, but we'll need to put on a bit of ssspeed. Now hhh-old on."

She gave her enormous wings a powerful flap, and dived into the clouds.

Back in Lerwick, the Indgar Vikings split up into search parties to look for Hel. One group checked the harbourside, another checked the town. Gertrude went off to check the local swamp, although everyone knew she was just looking for an excuse to collect creepy-crawly ingredients.

Velda, Grimm, Grut and Oswald, who was still in his

wheelbarrow, headed straight for the local inn. Inside, they found Hel slumped on the bar, snoozing over a flagon of mead. And who was sitting alongside him, topping up his drink from a big jug?

"Magnus!" growled Velda. "So that's your game!"

Magnus the Bone-Breaker grinned at them as he stood up, his posh armour gleaming in the light from the fire. Hel's head slumped forward, thumping on the table. He slowly rolled off the stool and crumpled to the floor in a heap.

"Dear, oh dear, oh dear!" laughed Magnus. "I heard a rumour that Hel the Dragonslayer's weakness was honeyed mead – it makes him sleepy. Looks like it was true! Well, whatever it is you lot are planning, it won't involve him."

"You'll never win, you overdressed snake!" snapped Velda.

"How are you and your crew of cretins going to stop me? I'm off to set my boat ablaze. They'll definitely make me the Guizer Jarl after seeing this." He barged out of the inn, laughter bellowing in his chest.

"All this sneaky business, it's SOOOO upsetting!" moaned Grimm.

"What are we going to do now?" asked Velda, staring down at the unconscious dragonslayer.

"I often find eating helps," said Grut, eyeing platters of meat being brought out of the kitchen.

Oswald gave a yawn. "Ooh, I could do with a nice lie-down myself." He promptly nestled down in his wheelbarrow and dozed off.

"Fat lot of good you are!" yelled Velda.

Then, from the corner of her eye, she caught a movement at the inn's window. Percy fluttered in, landed on Hel's chest and started pecking him on the breastplate. "Percy!" cried Velda. "That must mean Thorfinn's not far behind."

A tiny parcel dangled around the pigeon's neck. Velda unwrapped it to find a piece of paper, which she unfolded to reveal a message. "It's from Thorfinn! He's written instructions for our big show."

"But it's no good without Hel!" wailed Grimm.

"Wait! Thorfinn also sent this..." Velda held up a tiny packet of brown leaves. "He says it's his delightfully strong tea, in case Oswald needs perking up."

Grut stared at the old wise man who was now snoring loudly. "Tea may work for some, but a ham sandwich would do it for me."

"Forget Oswald! Let's use it to wake up Hel!" Velda tore open the packet and dropped a few of the tea leaves into a jug of warm water. Percy perched on the table and gazed into the jug, then up at Velda. He seemed to shake his tiny head.

"You're right, a bit more won't hurt..." Velda emptied in the whole packet, giving it a stir.

Grut held the dragonslayer's mouth open and Velda poured in the tea. For a moment, all they heard was a great glugging sound as the mixture rushed down the big man's gullet.

Exactly two seconds later, Hel's eyes shot open.

"RRRRRAAAARRRRGGH!"

Hel leapt in the air. His giant head, topped with his horned helmet, crashed through the roof. He hung there for a moment, legs swinging, until he pulled himself out and landed with a colossal **THUMP** on his huge feet.

"VVVVERY REFRESHING!"

"Oi!" Oswald sat up in his wheelbarrow and waved his fist at Hel. "Keep it down, you oversized numbskull. Can't you see I'm trying to nap?"

"OK," said Velda. "We've got Hel back, so what do we do now?"

"Magnus is moving fast," droned Grimm, pointing out the window towards the harbour. "Too fast! We're done for!"

"Then we'll just have to move even faster," said Velda. She grinned and kicked her roll-o-boots like a bull getting ready to charge.

CHAPTER 16

Outside, darkness had fallen, and the flaming torches of the Vikings lit up the night sky around the harbour.

Magnus the Bone-Breaker stepped up onto a big rock next to his longship. His men, dressed in their glimmering armour, formed a circle around the ship. They broke into a loud cheer, drawing the attention of the crowd.

Meanwhile, a short distance away, Erik the Ear-Masher was manning the gate to the cattle pen, gritting his teeth and clenching his fist. "Come on

Harald, give the order!" He gazed over at his chief, waiting for the nod to unleash the cattle. Suddenly something whizzed past his face, blowing off his helmet. "Hey!"

It was Velda, moving like a flash of lightning, ducking and swerving on her roll-o-boots through the crowd. "Out of my way, cretins!"

Harald spotted her from his position on the harbour wall, and he spotted Percy too, flying above. What he didn't spot was Grut and Grimm leading a tall hooded figure behind the crowd that surrounded Magnus's longship.

Velda screeched to a halt in front of Harald. "Chief! You've got to come with us!"

"Where to?" barked Harald. "Where's Hel?

Where's Thorfinn? And where's this blasted dragon?"

"I'll explain." She turned to Thorfinn's crew, who were gathered nearby. "You lot! Get changed into your costumes, fast!"

Velda led Harald and the others around the other side of Magnus's boat. And in the nick of time too, as at that moment Magnus lifted a huge war horn into the air and blew on it. Very loudly.

HONNNNKKK!

A great silence fell upon the crowd.

136

"Vikings!" Magnus roared. "Are you ready to witness the greatest Fire Festival spectacle you've ever seen?"

Hundreds of bellowing roars filled the air in response.

"YAAAAY!"

"YAAAAH"

"YIPPEEEE!"

"Then watch THIS!" He turned to his men. "Ready, lads?" Giving a triumphant laugh, Magnus raised his torch in the air, poised to start the show.

CHAPTER 17

At that very moment, the sea behind them seemed to rise up, and a deafening roar rumbled through the air. The Vikings stood open-mouthed and stared, terrified – even Magnus, who had been about to toss his flaming torch into the boat.

The water slowly cascaded away, revealing shiny red scales and spines, a set of sharp talons and piercing yellow eyes.

The crowd gasped. "The Great Dragon! HELP! SAVE US!"

Thorfinn was perched on the back of the dragon's

neck. He spat out some seawater, then leaned over and waved. "Hello! Lovely evening, isn't it?"

The Great Dragon flapped her giant wings and took to the night sky, soaring above the crowd and sending them into a panic.

"We have to make sure everyone stays to see our show!" barked Harald, waving over at Erik the Ear-Masher. Seeing the signal he'd been waiting for, Erik flung open the gate of the cattle pen. The cattle stampeded, sending up clouds of dust (and one or two stinky cowpats). They blocked the exits to the harbour, trapping the crowd inside.

Thorfinn leaned down and spoke quietly in Hazel's ear. "Ahem, could you do it now, dear friend?"

"Ffffor you – anything," replied Hazel. The dragon took a deep breath. Her tummy rumbled, then her nostrils erupted with flames. A giant stream of fire engulfed Magnus's longship.

Magnus and his men scattered, screaming.

Magnus himself, his bottom on fire, leapt into the harbour. "AAAAARGH!! MY BUM!!"

As the ship blazed, Hazel swooped to the ground behind it, lowering her head to let Thorfinn climb off.

Thorfinn doffed his helmet. "Thank you, Hazel. Now, would you mind awfully?"

"Of course not," replied Hazel. "What a polite little Thhh-orfinn you are!"

The dragon angled her head down and nudged a path through the middle of the longship's burning wreckage. As Hazel beat her wings and took to the air once more, Velda appeared at Thorfinn's side.

"Ready?" asked Thorfinn.

"You betcha!" Velda grinned and flashed her boots. The wheels were alight. "What do you think? I coated everything in that black oil and then set it on fire."

"Excellent idea, old pal," replied Thorfinn.

"How about me?" whined Oswald. The wheel of his rickety wheelbarrow was aflame. "Pretty cool – as you youths might say – don't you think?" He sounded a bit like an elderly penguin lying on a sun lounger trying a fancy cocktail.

"GO! GO! GO!" yelled Velda, and she skated

through the burning timbers.

One by one, the crew of the *Green Dragon* emerged from the longship. First Velda and her flaming roller boots, then Oswald in his fiery wheelbarrow, pushed by Grimm, moaning, "So this is how it ends – burned alive! Oh poor me!"

The rest of Thorfinn's crew followed in their sparkly suits.

Gertrude sashayed out like a teapot, with her arm stretched out. "Oooh, I is a star!"

Then came Grut, grumbling, "Do we get fed at the interval? I'm starving."

Next Harek leapt out, beaming with pride and winking at the crowd, which was a little bit scary given that both his eyes pointed in different directions.

"At last! I made it onto the big stage!"

Unfortunately, his big moment was short-lived because Torsten, who was following behind, crashed into him, and the two men tumbled off the burning boat.

"AAAARGH!"

SPLASH!

Even Olaf had agreed to dress up, but only because he'd rolled his costume in cattle dung so nobody could see the glitter. "I'd rather stink than sparkle!" he said grumpily.

Harald appeared last, his helmet horns blazing, looking every bit the giant, ferocious Viking chief.

As the dragon wheeled and glided above, breathing fire menacingly, the crowd called to Harald. "HELP! SAVE US!"

At that moment, Harald stepped to one side and beckoned out another figure from behind the burning ship, a huge Viking with broad, bull-like shoulders. Harald snatched the man's hand and thrust it into the air as the waiting Vikings realised...

"Hel! It's Hel the Dragonslayer! He'll save us!"

Hel pounced forward. Silhouetted against the flames, he was twice, or even three times the man he was before. He whipped out his massive sword and thrust it into the air, jabbing it in the direction of the circling dragon. "Now then, dragon!" he snarled. "Let us do battle! Just like the good old days!"

"Ohhh, goodie!" replied Hazel happily.

All the Vikings cheered. Except for Magnus,

whose mouth was full of seawater.

CHAPTER 18

With a rumble of happiness, Hazel dived from the sky and the battle began. Swooping low, she spewed flames over the rooftops. Hel replied by rigging up a makeshift catapult with a pair of Great Fire Festival souvenir underpants and firing cannonball-sized boulders.

"Too ssss-slow, dragonslayer!" hissed Hazel as she dodged his shots.

"I'll get you yet, dragon!" Hel roared back, loading up another boulder. He was thoroughly enjoying himself.

Their battle was one of the greatest duels any of the Vikings could remember. There wasn't much of old Lerwick left by the end, but the show was so good the townspeople didn't mind. When the last flames had been breathed and the last sword thrusts made, it was time for the dragon to leave. "Goodbye, Thhh-orfinn!" called Hazel as she banked away towards the sea. "And thhh-ank you!"

"No, thank you, old bean!" Thorfinn called back, doffing his helmet to her.

Hazel flew off across the open sea, while Hel rode out of town to the cheers of his fellow Vikings. Both dragon and dragonslayer had arranged to fight again regularly, on the third Wednesday of every month at about half-past two.

"LONG LIVE THE DRAGONSLAYER!" cried the Vikings.

As for Harald, he was carried aloft by the crowd to the podium, or what was left of it amidst the smoking ruins. He and his crew really had put on a spectacle the festival had never seen before.

"HARALD FOR GUIZER JARL!" they cried.

Standing proudly on top of a pile of ash and cinders, Harald was presented with his prize – a silver mace.

The first thing he did was to turn to his son, standing nearby with his crew.

"Here, my boy." Harald plonked the mace down in front of Thorfinn. "We won our bet with Magnus, and it's all thanks to you. This prize is yours. Besides..." Harald gazed over at his rival chief, who was slumped unhappily on a barrel, wringing seawater out of his hand-knitted socks. "I'm going to be a lot richer now I've won those thousand pieces!"

Thorfinn looked at the silver mace, scratching his chin. "Thank you, dear Dad, but it's rather large and heavy. I'm not sure I'll be able to lift it."

Harald boomed with laughter and hoisted both Thorfinn and the mace into the air. "Come on, son, I'll carry it for you!"

"So what are you going to do with it?" asked
Velda, as they made their way towards their ships.
"Sell it? Keep it as a trophy?"

"Oh, don't worry, dear pal, I know exactly what to
do with it," replied Thorfinn.

DAVID MACPHAIL left home at eighteen to travel the world and have adventures. After working as a chicken wrangler, a ghost-tour guide and a waiter on a tropical island, he now has the sensible job of writing about yetis and Vikings. At home in Perthshire, Scotland, he exists on a diet of cream buns and zombie movies.

RICHARD MORGAN was born and raised by goblins on the Yorkshire moors. After running away to New Zealand to play with yachts and paint backgrounds for Disney TV he returned to the UK to write and illustrate children's books. He now lives in Cambridge, England, and has a family of goblins of his own.

VIKING WORDSEARCH

B	R	E	S	E	L	A	C	S	H	T	R
O	A	T	R	E	A	S	U	R	E	E	E
O	D	R	A	G	N	O	W	C	Y	T	H
K	O	F	B	D	R	E	N	A	C	K	T
O	H	T	R	E	S	U	L	W	L	I	A
F	S	C	W	I	C	S	R	S	H	C	E
D	A	T	R	G	N	U	A	R	A	E	R
R	R	V	M	O	G	T	E	E	T	H	B
E	G	A	G	W	C	E	V	A	C	T	E
K	P	A	G	K	H	S	A	S	C	H	R
I	R	Z	B	O	F	J	C	L	A	E	I
D	A	R	S	G	N	I	W	R	E	T	F

DRAGON   WINGS   BOOK OF DREKI

DRAGONSLAYER   FIREBREATHER   SCORCH

BARBECUE   CLAWS   TREASURE

TEETH   SCALES   CAVE

DRAGON NAME GENERATOR

Follow these simple steps to find out your deadly dragon name!

1. What's your *first* name? The *first part* of your dragon name is exactly the same. Simple!

2. What *month* were you born? Use that to find the *second part* of your fiery title.

January: the Castle-Scorcher of...
February: the Helmet-Roaster of...
March: the Flame-Belcher of...
April: the Bridge-Melter of...
May: the Granny-Griller of...
June: the Ash-Farter of...
July: the Fire-Vomiter of...
August: the Bottom-Barbecuer of...
September: the Axe-Swallower of...
October: the Cave-Stinker of...
November: the Sky-Warrior of...
December: the Pants-Burner of...

3. *Where* were you born? Use that to find the *third part* of your awesome alias.

4. Add the three parts together

= YOUR DRAGON NAME!

FOR EXAMPLE: David MacPhail was born in May in Greenock so he becomes...

DAVID THE GRANNY-GRILLER OF GREENOCK

What's your deadly dragon name? What about your friends?

THE BOOK OF DREKI'S TOP 5 DRAGON-CARE TIPS

1. Dragons are **NOT** pets, but they do like a good scratch behind the ears and an occasional game of fetch. Give tummy tickles at your own peril.

2. It's important to feed your dragon a varied, balanced diet. If not, you might find that YOU become part of said varied, balanced diet. Avoid any SFEs (Stupid Feeding Errors) by wearing full body armour at feeding time.

3. Brushing a dragon's teeth requires the utmost care. **DO NOT** attempt to floss your dragon's fangs, unless you want to end up like Ulrick the Armless and Todrig the Crispy-Headed.

4. There are certain foods you must **NEVER** feed a dragon. Spaghetti, gingerbread and broccoli give dragons explosive wind. Noxious dragon bottom burps have been known to knock people unconscious for several weeks.

5. Dragons **DO NOT** like having their caves cleaned. If you must clean, use a VERY long-handled brush and find something to distract your dragon with (a snack-sized herd of oxen is ideal). Better still, wait until they've nipped out to burn the local village to the ground before spring-cleaning.

DISCLAIMER: Owners follow the above advice at their own risk. The Publisher accepts no liability for any dragon-related damage or injuries of any kind (dragon fart-induced comas included).

PERCY THE PIGEON POST

EST. 799AD   ODINSDAY 18TH FEBRUARY   PRICE: ONE FRONT TOOTH

SKULL-SPLITTING NEWS

In what will forever be known as the Awful Invasion the Scots have narrowly missed being invaded by a band of maurauding Vikings, led by the fearsome Chief of Indgar, Harald the Skull-Splitter.

SPORTING HEADLINES

It is the weekend of the annual Gruesome Games. Word on the beach is that Thorfinn and his motley team have to save their village from the clutches of Magnus the Bone-Breaker. Odds are on for a new Chief of Indgar by Monday.

FOULSOME FOOD

It's all about Le Poisson (that's FISH to you boneheads). The King of Norway is on his way to Indgar and he expects a most Disgusting Feast. But there's a poisoner at large and the heat is on in the kitchen...

TORTUROUS TRAVEL

Early booking is essential to visit the Rotten Scots' most famous prisoner (that's Thorfinn) at Castle Red Wolf. Hurry — he may be rescued at any moment!

LOST AND NOT FOUND

A massive hoard of Terrible Treasure stolen from the pesky Scots has mysteriously vanished. Large reward promised for information leading to its recovery.

MISSING PERSONS

The Raging Raiders are prime suspects in the kidnapping of one fed-up, goat-carrying Viking mum. Please report any sightings to Chief Harald the Skull-Splitter.

PUTRID POTION PLOT

Chief Harald has now been sleeping for several days, villagers have tried and failed to wake him. Thorfinn suspects a Putrid Potion may be behind the snoozy Skull-Splitter.

Collect all of Thorfinn's adventures